Especially for

----

from

----

*Goodnight and
God bless*

For blessings here
and those in store
we give thanks now
and evermore.

Written and compiled by Elena Pasquali
Illustrations copyright © 2013 Natascia Ugliano

This edition copyright © 2013 Lion Hudson

Published by Lion Children's Books
an imprint of
Lion Hudson plc
Wilkinson House, Jordan Hill Road,
Oxford OX2 8DR, England
www.lionhudson.com/lionchildrens

ISBN 978 0 7459 6389 1

First edition 2013

Acknowledgments
All unattributed prayers are by Elena Pasquali and Lois Rock, copyright © Lion Hudson.
Prayers by Christina Goodings and Sophie Piper are copyright © Lion Hudson.
Bible extracts are taken or adapted from the Good News Bible published by
the Bible Societies and HarperCollins Publishers, © American Bible Society 1994,
used with permission.
Prayer by Blessed Teresa of Calcutta used by permission.

A catalogue record for this book is available from the British Library

Printed and bound in Hong Kong, April 2013, LH33

Day is Done

Written and compiled by Elena Pasquali

Illustrated by Natascia Ugliano

LION
CHILDREN'S

Twilight

An evening prayer
as the sun sinks low:
we thank you, God,
for this world below.

An evening prayer
as the dark comes nigh:
we thank you, God,
for your heaven on high.

✛

I walk through daytime
flower by flower.
I'll dream through night-time
hour by hour,
for God will guard me
with his power
and be my shelter,
my high tower.

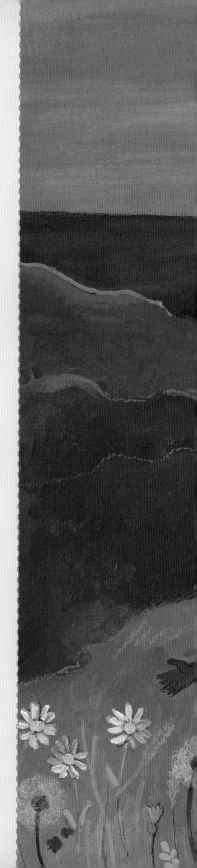

Thanksgiving

I sit still and quietly
in this, my quiet place,
and think of good and lovely things
and God's unfailing grace.

✣

Now the light is fading
and shadows turn to grey
I'll gather up my troubles
and fold them all away.
I'll gather all my blessings
and count them one by one
and dream away the night until
the rising of the sun.

At peace

With God you must let things begin,
With God let all things come to rest;
In this way the work of your hands
Will flourish and also be blessed.

Anonymous

✣

Dear God,
Help me to forget my mistakes but to
remember what they taught me.

✣

O Voice of Peace,
speak calm and clear
to heal each hurt,
to quiet each fear,
to guide each thought,
to bring sleep near
till dark night end
and light appear.

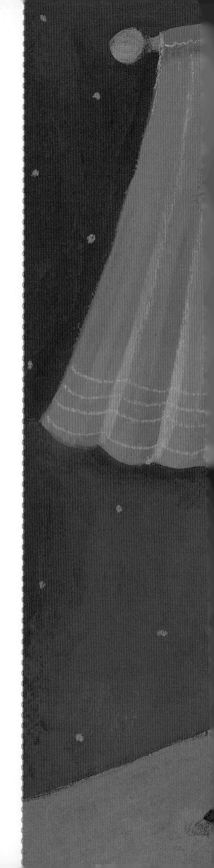

For those I love

God bless all those that I love;
God bless all those that love me;
God bless all those that love those
that I love,
And all those that love those that love me.

Anonymous

✢

Dear God, bless all my family,
as I tell you each name;
and please bless each one differently
for no one's quite the same.

The beauty of the night

I will give thanks for the darkness
for it is from the darkness
that everything in heaven and earth
was created.

✤

Open my eyes, dear God,
To the beauty of the night:
To a world of shape and silhouette,
And scatterings of silver.

✤

In the quiet night,
I can hear the wind
that blows from heaven,
bringing life and hope
to all the earth.

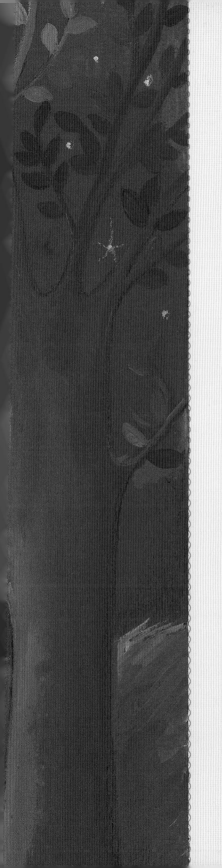

For night-time creatures

God bless the night-time creatures
in the shadows of the wood;
may they live their secret lives
as wild creatures should.

May they find their secret paths
through all the moonlit dark;
may they find their secret homes
when morning wakes the lark.

Moon and stars

I see the moon
And the moon sees me;
God bless the moon
And God bless me.

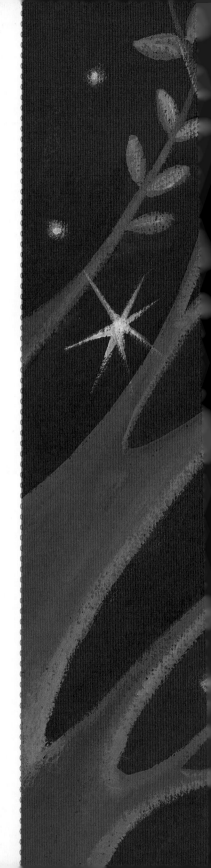

Traditional

✣

The world has turned to darkness
The sky has turned to night
The silver moon is promise of
The sun's returning light.
I turn my heart to thankfulness
I turn my thoughts to prayer.
I trust that heaven's angels
Are watching everywhere.

✣

The moon shines bright,
The stars give light
Before the break of day;
God bless you all
Both great and small
And send a joyful day.

Traditional

And so to bed

I lie down
and my home
is the shelter
of God's guarding.

I lie down
and my bed
is the comfort
of God's loving.

I lie down
and my sleep
is the peace
of angels watching.

✛

Now I lay me down to sleep,
I pray thee, Lord, thy child to keep;
Thy love to guard me through the night
And wake me in the morning light.

Traditional

The good shepherd

Kindly shepherd of the heavens,
lead your flock through fields of night
to the pool of deeply sleeping
and a dreamland of delight.

✤

Loving Shepherd of Thy sheep,
Keep Thy lambs, in safety keep;
Nothing can Thy power withstand;
None can pluck us from Thy hand.

Jane Eliza Leeson (1807–82)

✤

Dear God, you are my shepherd,
You give me all I need,
You take me where the grass grows green
And I can safely feed.

You take me where the water
Is quiet and cool and clear;
And there I rest and know I'm safe
For you are always near.

Based on Psalm 23

Heavenly angels

Lord, keep us safe this night,
Secure from all our fears;
May angels guard us while we sleep,
Till morning light appears.

John Leland (1754–1841)

✢

Clouds in the sky above,
Waves on the sea,
Angels up in heaven
Watching over you and me.

Christina Goodings

✢

Keep watch, dear God, with those who work,
or watch, or weep this night,
and give your angels charge over those
who sleep.

St Augustine (354–430)

Blessings

The blessing of the holy One
who gives me life to live
The blessing of the holy Son
who brings me love to give
The blessing of the holy One
who comes in wind and fire
to fill my life with joyfulness
and goodness to inspire.

Sophie Piper

✣

Deep peace of the running waves to you,
Deep peace of the flowing air to you,
Deep peace of the quiet earth to you,
Deep peace of the shining stars to you,
Deep peace of the shades of night to you,
Moon and stars always giving light to you,
Deep peace of Christ, the Son of Peace, to you.

Traditional Gaelic blessing

A new day

Morning is dawning
Creation awakening
The birds and the flowers and me.
We look to the sun
And we reach for the sky
To grow into all we should be.

✛

Father, lead us through this day,
the paths unknown, but blessed the way.

Sophie Piper

✛

We can do no great things,
Only small things with great love.

Blessed Teresa of Calcutta (1910–97)

This simply lovely day –
I want to share it.
There is no beauty with which
to compare it.
Each green, each blue,
each changing hue –
I hardly understand
how heav'n can spare it.